3013

D0264688

Bobby Dean
Saves Christmas

Bobby Dean
Saves Christmas

Illustrated by Rosie Brooks

ALED JONES

First published in Great Britain in 2021 by Hodder & Stoughton
An Hachette UK company

1

Copyright © Aled Jones, 2021
Illustrations © Rosie Brooks, 2021

The right of Aled Jones to be identified as the
Author of the Work has been asserted by him in accordance
with the Copyright, Designs and Patents Act 1988.

A CIP catalogue record for this title is available from the British Library

Hardback ISBN 978 1 529 37612 8
eBook ISBN 978 1 529 37614 2

Typeset in Sabon MT by
Palimpsest Book Production Ltd, Falkirk, Stirlingshire

Printed and bound in Great Britain by Clays Ltd, Elcograf S.p.A.

Hodder & Stoughton policy is to use papers that are natural, renewable
and recyclable products and made from wood grown in sustainable forests.
The logging and manufacturing processes are expected to conform
to the environmental regulations of the country of origin.

Hodder & Stoughton Ltd
Carmelite House
50 Victoria Embankment
London EC4Y 0DZ

www.hodderfaithyoungexplorers.co.uk

Contents

1
Off to School

Nine-year-old Bobby Dean was flying through the air on a carpet made entirely out of musical notes! To steer it, all he had to do was sing. A high note would make the carpet soar high above the clouds. A low note would have him skipping just above the trees. And if he sang a scale, he would loop-the-loop! It was amazing! Well, it was, until something pink and covered in slobbery drool fell out of the sky and donked him on his head.

Bobby peeled open his eyes. Sitting on his chest was a scruffy ginger dog, an enormous pink tongue lolling out of its mouth.

'Hi Ruff!' Bobby yawned. 'Time to get up?' Ruffian was Bobby's best friend. He barked and wagged his tail.

Bobby sat up and Ruffian jumped off the bed. On a chair by the wall, Bobby spotted his new school uniform and his enormous school bag. His stomach did a flip.

'It's my first day at school today, Ruff,' he said. 'Exciting, right?'

Ruffian cocked his head to one side then rested a large paw on Bobby's knee.

'Yeah, I'm a bit nervous,' Bobby said, convinced that his hairy pal could understand every word he said. 'But I'll be OK.'

Bobby had been homeschooled on his parents' farm, away from the rest of the world, but had now decided that he wanted to make new friends.

'This is a very grown-up decision,' Bobby's dad, Mr Dean, had said. 'Well done, Bobby!'

'We're very proud,' Bobby's mum, Mrs Dean, had said. 'Now, what about some pie?'

Bobby's mum always – ALWAYS – provided him with amazing food. 'One day, you'll shoot up so tall!' she would say. 'And it will be because of this marvellous chutney I've just made, I promise!' Or she would say, 'One day, you will be so strong! And it will be thanks to my tremendous meatloaf!'

The rich smell of bacon, eggs and mushrooms slipped into the room.

'Hungry?' Bobby asked Ruffian.

The dog answered by thumping his tail on the floor. 'First one there gets an extra sausage!' Bobby laughed and Ruffian zipped out of the bedroom, Bobby chasing after.

Racing into the kitchen, Bobby was confronted with great clouds of steam, the overwhelming delicious aroma of scrummy food, and the sound of his mum singing. Bobby didn't join in.

'Morning, Bean!' Bobby's mum said, calling him by the nickname she had given him when he was a baby, because he had been so small. Then she scrunched up her nose. She was a short woman with a big smile and rosy cheeks.

'Hmm,' she said, 'not singing today . . . You must be a little nervous about school. Breakfast will sort you out!'

Bobby tried to smile, but as he sat down his stomach did a little twist. Ruffian sat beside him and, once again, rested a paw on Bobby's knee.

'Nervous is good!' Bobby's dad said. He was a tall man with large hands and a beard that looked like a bird's nest.

'Is it?' asked Bobby.

'Of course!' Bobby's mum said. 'It means you're off on a new adventure! And you can't have a new adventure without being a little nervous, can you?'

Bobby shook his head. 'I suppose not, no.'

'Of course you can't!' Bobby's mum said. 'And singing always helps if you're feeling iffy for any reason at all, always remember that. Don't ever forget your voice, Bobby Bean! It's a little bit like magic!'

'Not if I sing, it isn't,' Bobby's dad said. 'I sound like a blocked drain!'

Everyone laughed.

Bobby's mum plonked down onto the table the biggest breakfast Bobby had ever seen – which was saying something, because Bobby's mum had made him some whoppers in her time! Bobby peered over the mountain of deliciousness at his mum.

'I made extra because it's a special day!' she said. 'Sausage, eggs, bacon, mushrooms, fried bread, beans, fried potatoes. And a large glass of homemade milkshake!'

'Not sure there's enough on that plate,' Bobby's dad laughed. 'I mean, I can actually still see some of the plate.'

'He's a growing boy,' said Bobby's mum. 'He won't always be a little bean, you know. Some day, we'll wake up, and he'll be a beanstalk, taller than all of us! And you know why?'

'Do tell,' said Bobby's dad.

'Because of this very breakfast, that's why! And the roast we had yesterday. That as well, obviously. And my jam. That's very special.'

'This is true,' Bobby's dad replied, winking at Bobby, 'but I don't think he has to do all of his growing in one go, do you?'

After breakfast, Bobby walked down the lane from the farm to the road to wait for the school bus. Sitting by his side, Ruffian stared up at him, his tail thumping up a little tornado of dust.

'No dogs allowed in school, pal,' said Bobby, his voice wobbling a little. 'Especially scruffy barking-mad ones, like you! Off you go back to the farm, and I'll see you later, yeah?' Ruffian nuzzled

into Bobby's legs. Bobby squatted down and gave the dog a massive squeezy hug. 'Love you, Ruff,'

Bobby said, then off the dog ran, back down the lane, to where Bobby could see his mum and dad still watching from the house.

He waved, to show them he was brave, but it didn't stop his legs feeling like jelly.

8

'You can do this, Bobby Dean!' he muttered to himself. 'You can do this!' Then, from somewhere down the lane, Bobby heard music and the clattering rattle of the old school bus.

You can do this!

2

Legin's Bouncy Bus

B obby stepped back as the bouncing school bus slowed to a stop. The door squeaked open. Sitting behind the wheel was a man with long black hair and a long black beard. He was wearing a huge black, red, yellow and green cap, a black leather jacket and ripped jeans. Bobby thought his bright green dark glasses made him look really cool.

'Hello, Bobby Dean!' the driver beamed. 'My name's Legin. You like reggae music?'

'Yes,' Bobby nodded, having never heard anything like it before in his life.

'Well come on up, then!' Legin cheered. 'And get yourself into the fun bus!'

Bobby lifted a foot, then hesitated. He glanced back down the lane to his house. His parents were there still, Ruffian with them. They waved and he waved back.

'Be quick now,' Legin laughed, 'because this next track is jumpin'', little man!'

Bobby climbed up into the bus and for a moment it felt like the music was lifting him. He glanced up the bus at a sea of new faces, then quickly took his seat behind Legin.

'Feel the rhythm, feel the rhyme, stay in your seats, it's schooling time!' Legin bellowed over the music. Everyone cheered! Well, everyone except Bobby.

'I'll just pretend I'm invisible,' he thought, and

watched through the window as the bus pulled away
from the farm.

At long last, the bus arrived at the school. The door
hissed open. A man the size of a mountain climbed
up the steps. He was dressed in a brown tweed
jacket and had an enormous white moustache.
Bobby thought that the man looked like a walrus.
Though this walrus was wearing a kilt and Bobby
tried not to stare at the man's very hairy knees.

'Good morning, everyone!' the man boomed in a
Scottish accent.

'Good morning,
Mr Morris!' everyone but
Bobby replied.

Mr Morris turned to Bobby and
smiled wide.

'Well, hello there, Bobby Dean!
Excited about your first day at school?'

'I don't know,' Bobby replied. 'I
think so.'

Mr Morris ordered everyone off the bus and then
led Bobby into the school.

The sunlight reflecting in the huge glass windows
lit up the bright blue colour of the school quite
brilliantly. It was all shiny as if it had just been
polished, and was by far the biggest building Bobby
had ever seen. Walking in through the enormous
main doors into the main hall with its high ceilings
made him feel a little bit sick. Then he smelled
something delicious, which reminded him of home
and his mum's wonderful cooking.

'It's roast chicken for lunch!' declared Mr Morris. 'You've chosen a good day to join us, Bobby.'

'Roast potatoes, too,' thought Bobby, sniffing the air. 'Yum!'

Mr Morris led Bobby through to his office and handed him a glass of squash. He then sat behind his desk and picked up a book.

Bobby read the title: *World's Worst Jokes.*

'So, Bobby,' Mr Morris said, 'can you tell me why farts never graduate from school?'

Bobby didn't know what to say or where to look and just shook his head.

'Because they end up getting expelled! Hahahaha!'

Mr Morris's laugh bounced around the room like a huge inflatable ball.

'Now that's comedy, Bobby!'

Bobby laughed. He couldn't help himself. Mr Morris really was quite funny.

'Not that you'd ever get expelled, hey, Bobby?'

Mr Morris gave Bobby a playful nudge, which nearly sent him flying.

'I don't know my own strength,' Mr Morris said. 'Highland Games caber tossing champion for the last two years, you see.'

Mr Morris pointed Bobby to a photo hanging on the wall. In it, the head teacher was wearing a kilt and carrying a massive tree with no branches. He looked very sweaty, Bobby thought.

Mr Morris tapped a finger on another photo, this one of him playing rugby. 'That was my first cap for Scotland,' he said. 'Now, tell me, how's your mum? We used to be classmates back in the day, you know.'

'Really?' Bobby said.

'And I bet she still sings all the time, am I right? What a wonderful voice she had! Magical! I hope you sing, too, Bobby, yes?'

'I do, a little,' Bobby said.

'Marvellous! Then your first task this week is to audition for the school nativity!'

'Audition?' Bobby said. 'But I've never sung in front of people before! Only Mum and Dad, and Ruffian!'

'Ruffian?'

'He's our dog,' Bobby said.

'Well, if you can sing for a dog, you can sing for anyone, wouldn't you agree?'

Bobby didn't know what to say, so said nothing.

'Fabulous! Now, let's get you to your class. You have an exciting day ahead. Come on!'

'And by the way, "class" doesn't stand for "Come Late And Start Sleeping"!'

Bobby rolled his eyes and groaned at another of Mr Morris's jokes.

Mr Morris walked Bobby along a very long grey corridor. It seemed to go on for ever and ever. Bobby felt like the walls were closing in, the grey paint dripping off the walls. He peeked through windows and saw lots of children busy at work.

Ahead, Bobby saw a thin man with a bald head.

He was wearing grey overalls and he was mopping the floor.

'Morning, Finch,' said Mr Morris. 'The school smells nice and clean, good job!'

'Thank you, sir,' Mr Finch said, his voice a strange, high whisper. 'Kids are messy things, though. Always so messy!'

Mr Morris hurried them on past Mr Finch who continued to whisper to himself, complaining about children being messy.

'Here we are, Bobby!' said Mr Morris, coming to a stop at a classroom door. 'Time for you to meet your new friends!'

Bobby stepped into the room, holding his breath. The classroom fell silent and 30 strange faces turned to look at him. Bobby could hear his heart beating like a drum.

'But everyone and everywhere is so big!' Bobby muttered to himself, staring at the class and thinking about the school. 'I should have stayed on the farm where I was safe!'

Then his stomach started to churn, and all Bobby

really wanted to do was run back home. But he couldn't do that. He just needed to calm down. But how? What could he do?

Then Bobby remembered what his mum had said at breakfast: *Singing always helps, remember that. Don't ever forget your voice, it's a little bit like magic!*

So, Bobby started to sing. And as his voice slipped out into the day, he noticed something strange was happening. First there was a tingle in his toes, then a shiver up his spine, and finally a very bright light!

'Well, this is strange,' Bobby thought. Then there was a sound like flutes and songbirds and running water. And then the classroom disappeared.

3

Scruff Island

Bobby spun and rolled in a darkness so thick he couldn't see his hand in front of his face as it came up to bonk him on the nose. He spun some more, did a back flip, then his other hand whooshed in, out of control, and poked him in the eye!

'Ouch!'

A moment ago, Bobby had been walking into his new classroom, but now? Well, he hadn't the faintest idea what was happening, but it was all very exciting indeed! Far off, Bobby spotted a blob of bright swirling colours, and he was picking up speed, rushing towards it now, faster and faster! His ears popped and he heard a deafening high-pitched 'zip' sound. Then silence. He was no longer moving.

'Where on earth am I?' Bobby muttered, rubbing his eyes.

'Scruff Island, mate,' a growly voice replied. 'Last on anyone's list of holiday destinations, that's for sure.'

A revolting stench drifted up Bobby's nose and into his mouth. It reminded him of Ruffian's breath after he'd eaten some cow poop a few weeks ago, only worse. Bobby looked around to see that he was sitting on a craggy, grassy lump with a view of the sea. The weather was grey and cold.

Something soft brushed against Bobby's face. He

opened his eyes to see a mountain of scruffy golden hair, like a pile of straw. It was a dog so tall that he looked straight into Bobby's eyes.

'I'm Daggy,' the dog growled, 'But you can call me Dag.'

'You're a dog,' Bobby said.

'What gave it away?' Dag replied. 'The ears? The nose? My four legs and tail?'

'But you talk,' Bobby said. 'You're a dog and you talk, and dogs don't talk, do they?'

'Well, they do on Scruff Island, mate!' Dag said. 'Let me introduce you to my pack.'

Three dogs came to stand beside Dag. The first,

a small brown dog, the shape of a large sausage, stepped forward.

'Pleased to meet you!' the dog said, its voice a high-pitched yap. 'I'm Pip! Who are you? Where are you from? What's your favourite bone? Do you like biscuits? I love biscuits! And hotdogs. Do you like hotdogs? I've not had a hotdog in months! Did you bring any with you? I hope so. Give us a hotdog!'

'You've a high voice, but you're low to the ground,' Bobby laughed.

'And he never stops yapping,' growled Dag. 'Give it a rest, will ya, Pip?'

Next to Pip, Bobby saw a dog covered in patches of white and ginger hair. It was zooming round and around, chasing its tail.

'That's Fly,' said

Dag, shaking his head. 'She's the fastest dog on the island, right enough, but she's also just a little bit crazy!'

'Hey, Bobby!' Fly said, still spinning. 'I'd shake you by the paw, but I'm a bit busy right now! Come here, tail! Come here!'

The last dog was standing on its own, watching. It was covered in hair as shiny and black as oil, Bobby thought.

'That's Dink,' Dag  said. 'She's the brains of the team. Keeps herself to herself but is kind and will always fetch anything you need.'

Dink raised a paw as if to wave at Bobby, who waved back.

'Why are you on this island?' Bobby asked, looking at the four dogs in front of him. 'Who looks after you?'

Fly stopped chasing her tail. 'Who looks after us? No one, that's who!' she growled. 'We're prisoners.'

'Prisoners?' Bobby said. 'But you're dogs! Who would keep dogs as prisoners?'

'Lord Dampnut keeps us prisoners, that's who,' Dag said.

'Lord Dampnut? Who's he?' asked Bobby.

'He's someone who only loves perfect dogs,' Dag explained.

'Ain't a fan of us slightly scruffy mutts,' Dink said, gnawing at her words. 'Dogs who aren't pedigree.'

Dag leaned in close to Bobby, who held his breath, just in case. 'If you want to see Dampnut at work, we'll show you,' he said. 'But you'll have to be as still as a mouse in Catland!'

'I'm small and good at hiding,' Bobby said.

'Then move fast and stay low,' Dag said. 'And follow me.'

Dag crept off, with Pip, Fly and Dink following him. Bobby came along last, moving as quietly as he could, crawling along the ground. Dag led them along a small path then through some very long grass, which waved and danced in the wind, until finally they all came to a stop on top of a small hill.

'Everyone still now,' Dag said. 'Heads down, stay hidden, and don't move a muscle.'

At the bottom of the hill was a little cove with a pebbly beach. Pulled up on the beach was a boat. In the cove Bobby saw two men talking, their voices drifting up to him. One was dressed in a long black coat, which reached down to his boots. On his head he wore a black hat. He was thin and tall like a telegraph pole, Bobby thought. The other man was large and round, and dressed in a suit with a waistcoat that looked as though at any moment it would burst open.

'Evening, Lord Dampnut,' said the man in the black coat, his voice low, like rumbling thunder. 'Sorry we're late. Sea was rough.'

The other man was silent for a moment. So, that's Lord Dampnut, Bobby thought.

'Well, you're here now so let's get on with it,' Dampnut said. His voice was a thin whine, like air being let out of a balloon. 'I'm very important, you know. And important people, like me, are busy people. We are busy, important people who love being important and busy. Which I am! So, get a move on, please!'

'Yes, my lord,' the man replied and returned to the boat, before coming back to Lord Dampnut dragging behind him a huge sack.

Bobby stared at the sack. It was moving.

'New arrivals,' Dag said. 'Taken from their homes and their owners.'

Dink growled quietly. 'He thinks the only dogs worth having are ones that don't look like us, if you know what I mean,' she said. 'Neat and tidy and perfect.'

'And expensive,' yapped Pip.

'This is horrible,' Bobby said, a knot twisting his stomach. 'We have to do something!'

'We've tried to escape once,' Fly whimpered. 'But Dampnut nearly caught us and now he knows who we are. If we tried again and he got his hands on us, there's no knowing what he would do.'

'We really miss our owners,' Pip said. 'All the dogs on the island do. It's horrible here.'

Dag said, 'We need to be home for Christmas,

Bobby. So that we can be with our families. This, well, none of it is right, is it?'

'No, it's not right at all,' Bobby said, and found himself thinking of his best friend Ruffian at home on the farm. Christmas without him would be terrible and just didn't bear thinking about. And these dogs were just like Ruff, weren't they? They needed to get home, to be with the people who loved them and would look after them.

'I'm going to help you,' Bobby said, looking at each of the dogs in turn. 'I'm going to help you stop Dampnut and together we're going to get every single dog on Scruff Island back home for Christmas!'

Dink came over to Bobby and licked his nose. 'Thank you!' she said. 'But right now, we need to move! It's getting dark and Dampnut will be out soon to try to find us.'

'We need to get to our den,' Pip said. 'It's deep in the forest. Dampnut will never find us there.'

'But how will I get there?' Bobby asked. 'You're

dogs and you can run fast. I'm just me. I'll never keep up!'

Dag rested a paw on Bobby's shoulder. 'Jump on my back, Bobby, and hold on tight!'

4

The Great Escape

Bobby woke up with Dag hitting him in the face with his paws.

'Run, everyone! Run!' Dag woofed.

Bobby shook Dag. 'Wake up, Dag! You're having a nightmare!'

Dag sat up and stared at Bobby. They were huddled together with Pip, Fly and Dink, on an old blanket in the den, as tight as five spoons stuck together in the cutlery drawer at home.

'Sorry,' Dag growled. 'Was I snoring? I usually snore.'

'He does,' Pip said. 'It's very loud. Sometimes I think it's the ghost of Scruff Island!'

'There's a ghost?' Bobby asked.

'Oh, yes,' Dag yawned. 'An old sailor, wrecked on the shore centuries ago. They say he walks the island looking for his boat, trying to get home!'

'That's really creepy!' Bobby said. 'Anyway, you weren't snoring, you were dreaming.'

Dag gave a nod. 'Lots on my mind.'

'We all have,' said Dink.

The dogs all nodded.

After seeing Lord Dampnut, the dogs had taken
Bobby to their den to plan what they were going to
do. They had all been so tired that sleep had
overtaken them. Now though, with dusk creeping
across the island, they were awake again.

'Best we get ready,' Dink said, and led everyone
over to a map she had drawn earlier on the dusty
floor of the den. 'As you saw last night, Bobby, this
is where the new dogs are brought to the island by
boat.'

Bobby stared down at the map where Dink's
paw was resting on a drawing of the jetty and the
boat. 'And Dampnut just leaves you here?' he asked.

'This island is a dumping ground,' Fly said. 'No
one here is ever meant to go home.'

'Well, we're about to change all that, aren't we?'
Bobby said, and ruffled the fur on Fly's back.

'I hope so,' Pip whimpered. 'But I'm only small,
and it's going to be really, really dark . . .'

'Rubbish!' Bobby said. The word came out of his
mouth before he had a chance to stop it. 'I'm small

and I know we can beat Dampnut! We're an amazing dog-and-boy team!'

'But the dark . . .' Pip said.

'Is nothing to be afraid of,' Bobby said, 'when you're with friends!'

'That's it, Bobby!' Dag barked and gently rested a paw on Pip's head. 'We're a team!'

Dink and Fly both barked in agreement.

'Now, back to the plan,' Dink said. 'Are you sure you all know what needs to be done? Fly?'

Fly sat up to attention.

'I'm to bite Lord Dampnut on the bum! It's a tough job, but I'll take one for the team!'

Everyone smiled.

'Pip?'

'Easy, boss! I'll go for the ankles. I'll trip him up good and proper!'

'Dag?' Dink asked. 'You got your dancing paws on? And have you made sure all the dogs on the island know to come running once you give the sign?'

'Certainly have, I've got the mutt moves! And all the dogs know the drill.'

Dink then looked at Bobby and raised an eyebrow. 'Well?'

'Let's go!' Bobby said.

The dogs woofed and howled in excitement.

When they arrived at the jetty, the night was thick with darkness, the stars hidden from sight. The wind howled around them like a hyena, whipping stinging rain into Bobby's face.

'I'm soaked to the skin,' Pip complained.

The dogs and Bobby stared down to where Lord

Dampnut's boat was tied. To Bobby, it seemed to be alive, shaking violently from side to side, banging against the wooden deck, like it was trying to escape.

The boat's captain walked out onto the deck.

'We're here, my lord,' he said with a bow. 'That was a rough crossing.'

Lord Dampnut joined the captain on the deck, his round belly pushing out through his jacket.

Bobby laughed. 'He looks like a huge ugly seal!'

Dink lifted a paw. 'Time to see a man about a dog! Move it, Dag!'

Dag leapt up onto the jetty then bounded up and onto the boat. He crept up behind the captain and Dampnut, then started to dance.

'Hey, beanpole! Hey soaked-nut! Check me out, I'm the hip-hop hound!' Dag shook his tail, kicked his paws in the air, and even managed to do a back flip!

'Get out of here!' Lord Dampnut shouted. 'Or I'll have you skinned to make me a new coat!'

Dag kept on dancing.

'Right, now it's our turn,' Dink said.

With the captain distracted, Bobby, Dink, Fly and Pip crept their way up and onto the jetty, and onto the boat.

Bobby noticed some old wet clothes lying on the floor of the boat. And there was a torch lying close by. Then he remembered the story about the ghost of Scruff Island. 'I've an idea!' he said, picking up the large pair of black trousers. 'Pip! Fly! Up onto my shoulders! Quick!'

Dink bared her teeth in a smile. 'Great idea!' she said. 'Come on, you two, do as he said!'

Bobby pulled on the trousers then Pip and Fly jumped up onto his shoulders.

'Pass that old coat up,' Bobby said to Dink, and he pulled it over himself, Pip and Fly. 'Now the hat!'

Dink threw the hat to Fly who put it on her head.

'Right,' Bobby said, 'when I say, I want you both to howl! Can you do that? And make it really, really creepy!'

'Why?' Fly asked.

'Because we're the ghost of Scruff Island,' Bobby said, 'and we have some haunting to do!'

Bobby, Pip and Fly walked to the back of the boat and slowly up towards Lord Dampnut and the captain. They were still too busy watching Dag dance.

The darkness split with a sudden crack of thunder and bright lightning.

'Now!' said Bobby.

Dink clicked on the torch. Fly and Pip started to howl.

'I am the ghost of Scruff Island!' Bobby bellowed. 'And I've come for your boat!'

Lord Dampnut turned to face Bobby, Pip and Fly. 'You're . . . you're a ghost!' he cried, as his face drained of all colour.

47

'Give me your boat,' Bobby said, 'or I'll haunt you forever!'

'And make you chase your tail every day!' added Pip.

'I might even bite your butt!' finished Fly.

The captain screamed with fright.

'Come here and let me get a good bite!' Fly growled.

'WoooOOOoooo!' Bobby moaned.

'You're on your own, Dampnut!' the captain screamed, then he jumped off the boat and into the sea.

Dag howled and the sound of it cut through the wind and the rain.

'Dink! Look!' Bobby said, and pointed out into the darkness.

Running towards them from all directions were hundreds of dogs.

Lord Dampnut was frozen to the spot. 'Don't come any closer!' he shouted.

The dogs took no notice, racing closer and closer.

'Time to give me your boat!' Bobby said. His voice caught and twisted in the wind. 'Now!'

Dampnut squealed then tried to jump off the boat. But his trousers caught on a nail, which ripped a huge hole in them, and he toppled into the water.

'Check out those spotty pants!' Bobby pointed, as Lord Dampnut waddled as fast as he could away into the darkness. The dogs laughed and barked as Lord Dampnut's spotty bum finally disappeared out of sight.

A few minutes later, the boat was covered in dogs.

'Anyone know how to steer this thing?' Dink asked.

Bobby stepped forward. 'I'll do it,' he said. 'Hold on, everyone!'

'But what about Dampnut?' Pip barked, as the boat pulled away from the jetty.

'He's still lord of Scruff Island,' Dag laughed. 'But without his boat, dogs are safe once more!'

All the dogs on the boat began to howl and bark as Bobby steered them away from the island.

'You kept your promise,' Dag said. 'We'll all be home for Christmas. Thanks, Bobby!'

'Hurrah for Bobby!' Pip woofed, and every dog on the boat let out a howl of joy.

'Join in!' Dink said to Bobby. 'I'm sure you can howl with happiness, too!'

Bobby laughed. 'I can't howl, but I can certainly sing,' he said, and joined in with a tune.

Then it happened again. There was a tingle in his toes, a shiver up his spine, and then a very high-

pitched 'zip' sound once again. This time he was
being hurled back through
the blob of bright
swirling colours. He was
spinning, and forward
rolling again through
total darkness. He
couldn't see a thing
except the flashing of
distant stars.

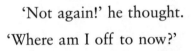

'Not again!' he thought.
'Where am I off to now?'

He shut his eyes and heard a sound like flutes and
songbirds and running water. Then silence. The
smell of roast chicken tickled Bobby's nose. Then he
opened his eyes and found himself back in the
classroom.

5

Bobby Meets the Gang

'Hello, Bobby!' Miss Evans smiled. 'Come on in and meet your new class. And was that you singing? You have a wonderful voice!'

Bobby gulped. He remembered singing because he was nervous. Then he had found himself on Scruff Island. And now he was back here! What on earth was going on?

'In you go, then, Bobby,' said Mr Morris, the head teacher. 'Nothing to be nervous about. Miss Evans' bark is worse than her bite!'

Bobby heard Mr Morris close the classroom door as Miss Evans walked over to meet him.

'Right then, everyone,' Miss Evans said, turning to the class, 'I want you to all give Bobby Dean here a great big welcome to the class. Ready?'

Bobby watched as everyone sat up straight in their chairs. They all sat in groups around red and blue tables.

'Now!' Miss Evans said.

Suddenly, everyone was out of their chair and doing a little dance. They were all clapping and spinning and foot-tapping and cheering. One boy even did a back flip! Bobby remembered Dag doing the same on Scruff Island. Had it all been a dream? How could he have been to an island of stray dogs and still be here, at school? It didn't make sense!

'Stop!' said Miss Evans, her voice firm and clear.

Everyone stopped dancing and sat back on their chairs.

'Douglas?'

The boy Bobby had seen do a back flip stood up. He was tall and scruffy and reminded Bobby of Dag.

'Yes, Miss Evans?'

'I'd like you and your friends to look after Bobby and show him around. Can you do that?'

'Absolutely!' Douglas said. 'Come on, Bobby! Over here to join the awesome crew.'

Bobby walked over and sat next to Douglas.

'Miss calls me Douglas, but everyone calls me Doug,' the boy said.

Bobby looked at the other children around the table.

'I'm Polo,' said a boy sitting next to Doug. He was no taller than himself, Bobby noticed.

'I've not heard that name before,' Bobby said.

'It's African for alligator!' Polo grinned. 'Nice to have someone here who sees eye to eye with me. Ha!'

'You remind me of someone,' Bobby said, looking at the group of children sitting with him. 'In fact, you all do!'

'You hungry?' Polo asked. 'It's roast chicken today. Tomorrow is hotdogs, my favourite.'

'That's it!' Bobby said. 'You're just like Pip!'

'You mean there's someone else as awesome as me?' Polo asked.

Bobby was about to say something about Scruff Island when the classroom door banged open.

'That'll be Dash,' Doug said.

Bobby turned and saw a girl with ginger hair standing in the doorway. She was wearing a tracksuit and trainers.

'Fastest kid in the school,' Doug explained. 'Always dresses like that.'

'Considering the fact that you run everywhere, you do seem to arrive late an awful lot,' Miss Evans said, staring at the ginger-haired girl. 'So, what is today's reason, Sasha?'

'I've been chasing my tail all

morning, Miss,' Dash said, 'training, then trying to find my homework. Found it though, so all's cool!'

Dash walked over to Bobby's table and sat down. 'New kid?' she said.

'This is Bobby,' said Doug.

'Hi,' said Bobby and raised a hand.

'Nice voice, by the way,' said the remaining member of the group, a girl with a high ponytail.

'Thanks,' said Bobby. 'I think. I mean, I sing when I'm nervous sometimes. Bit embarrassing.'

'No, it isn't,' the girl said. 'Singing rocks! I'm Katinka.'

'Tink for short, right?' Bobby said, thinking then how she reminded him of Dink.

'It's a Russian name,' Katinka said. 'And yes, it is Tink. Good guess!'

'Oh, no, not again!' Miss Evans sighed, and everyone turned to see her looking at the large interactive whiteboard at the front of the class.

'Need some help, Miss?' Tink asked.

Bobby watched as Tink walked over to Miss Evans. A moment or two later and the whiteboard was working again.

'Tink is head of the school computer group, too,' Polo said.

'So, what do you think, then?' Doug asked. 'Happy to be here?'

'With the awesome crew?' Bobby smiled. 'I think so, yes!'

Polo grinned. 'You're part of the gang now. No escape!'

'Unless you can run faster than me, that is,' said Dash.

'Do you sing a lot?' Tink asked.

'Yes,' Bobby nodded. 'It's not very cool, I know.'

'It's super cool, actually,' Tink said, then put her hand in the air. 'Miss Evans?'

'Yes, Katinka?'

'Will you be wanting someone to do a solo in the nativity this year?'

'Are you volunteering?' Miss Evans asked.

'No, but Bobby is!' Tink said. 'Aren't you, Bobby?'

'Am I?'

'Yes!' cheered the rest of the gang.

'Well?' Miss Evans said, looking at Bobby. 'Would you like to?'

Bobby looked at his new friends. They were all smiling at him and clapping. He stood up. 'Yes, Miss Evans,' Bobby said. 'I would!'

 Bobby woke on Saturday morning to the sound of sizzling bacon. His favourite smell was wafting up the stairs from the kitchen. The week had zipped by quicker than Dash doing the one hundred metres. And Bobby wasn't sure what had been more exciting, the rescue on Scruff Island or meeting his new friends and starting school.

'Morning, Ruff!' he said, as the dog gave him a

slobbery lick. 'What's the bet Mum has cooked the biggest breakfast ever?'

Bobby threw on his dressing gown.

'Let's go find out, shall we, Flea Bag?'

Dad looked up from the morning paper as Bobby and Ruffian skidded into the kitchen.

'Morning, Bobby! Hope you're hungry, because your mum thinks she's feeding an army again!'

'He's definitely grown this last week,' said Bobby's mum, putting a hefty plateful down on the table. 'So, he needs feeding even more!'

Bobby and his dad looked at each other and smiled.

'It's been the best week ever,' said Bobby, 'I love school so much! And Mr Morris the head teacher is so funny. Even Miss Evans laughs at his jokes. And she's quite serious! I told you about Legin, right? The rapping bus driver? And the solo in the nativity?'

'No, I haven't heard about any of that,' Bobby's dad said, rolling his eyes. 'It's not like you haven't talked about school all week!'

'I've loved hearing about all your new friends, too,' said Bobby's mum.

Bobby stared at the food in front of him:

sausages; bacon; two eggs; hash browns; mushrooms; tomatoes; fried bread; buttered bread; beans; and just for good measure, a slice of black pudding!

Ruffian licked his nose in anticipation of at least a bit of bacon.

A loud knock from the front door echoed through the house.

'Wonder who that is?' said Bobby's mum.

Ruffian wagged his tail and ran to the front door, followed closely by Bobby with a sausage between his fingers.

Bobby opened the door.

'Hey, Bob! Happy Saturday!'

Bobby stared out of the door, the sausage halfway to his mouth. There, in front of him, were his new friends from school!

'It's the gang!' shouted Bobby.

Bobby's mum and dad arrived at the door.

'Hello!' Bobby's mum smiled and held out a hand to reveal a large plate of sausages and bacon. 'Have a sausage!'

Bobby's friends all reached for the plate.

'Thanks, Mrs D!' said Doug, stuffing a sausage into his mouth.

'Well, you lot have fun today,' Bobby's dad said. 'And we'll see you back here for lunch.' Bobby's parents walked back into the house.

'So, what's the plan?' asked Tink. 'I love a plan! Plans are the best.'

Bobby thought for a moment, then a grin slipped across his face. 'You know what we need, don't you?' he asked.

'More sausages?' said Dash.

'Bacon!' said Polo.

Bobby laughed. 'A den!'
he said, and Ruffian barked in
agreement.

'But where?' Doug asked.

'We've got a little woodland on the
farm,' Bobby said, finishing his
sausage and stepping out into
the day, closing the door behind him. 'Come on!'

Before anyone could stop him, Bobby ran across
the yard in front of the house, climbed over a little
stile and into a meadow, and dashed ahead towards
some trees, Ruffian running alongside him. And as
he disappeared underneath the branches of a huge
ancient oak tree, the day wrapped itself around him
with the sound of laughter from his new friends
following along behind.

6

Mr Finch and the Nativity Rehearsals

'Come on, you lovely lot!' Miss Evans said, clapping her hands. 'We haven't got all day! This nativity show isn't going to direct itself! First positions, please!'

Bobby's first term at school was going so fast. The whizz, bang and crash sounds of fireworks from Bonfire Night had flown past, and all efforts were now being put into the Christmas show. Bobby was on stage with the rest of the cast.

'I was Juliet in *Romeo and Juliet*,' said Miss

Evans, lost in a world of her own. 'The village is still talking about my performance!'

Bobby took off his winter coat and walked to the front of the stage. He had the honour of opening the show.

'Lights, Katinka!' shouted Miss Evans.

Bobby started to sing.

'Once in royal David's city, stood a lowly cattle shed . . .'

'Wonderful,' said Miss Evans, a tear in her eye.

A shout from Tink interrupted the performance, followed by a fizzing sound and a flash of sparks.

'The lighting desk, Miss!' she said. 'Something's wrong!'

'What's wrong?' Miss Evans asked.

'It's buzzing!'

A loud bang shook the hall. Then darkness.

'Oh dear,' said Miss Evans.

The room fell silent.

A creaking sound crept through the room.

'What's that?' Bobby asked, hearing something in the gloom.

The squeaking crept closer and closer to the stage.

'This is well creepy!' said Dash.

'Turn the lights on, Tink!' shouted Polo.

'I'm trying to!' Tink replied from somewhere in the dark, fiddling with the lighting board. 'This should work . . .'

The room burst with a bright white light.

Bobby blinked then saw that standing next to him

on stage was a thin figure with a head as shiny and bald as a balloon.

'Yikes!' Bobby yelled, then realised it was Mr Finch, the caretaker. He was clutching some sheet music in his bony fingers.

'Can we help you, Mr Finch?' asked Miss Evans, just as the school bell rang for lunch.

Mr Finch glanced at Bobby, opened his mouth like he was about to say something, then turned and left.

'What was that all about?' asked Doug, as Bobby and the rest of the gang made their way out of the hall, the air filled with delicious smells.

Bobby thought for a moment. 'I think he wanted to join in,' he said.

'Finch?' Dash said. 'No way!'

Bobby shrugged. 'Maybe I was wrong, but I think that's what he wanted, yes.'

'No point worrying about it,' Polo said. 'Not when there are hotdogs that need eating. Come on!'

On the journey home later that day, Bobby was crushed up with his new friends on the back seat of the old school bus like sardines in a tin. Doug was taking up the most space and Tink was trying to read a lighting manual while sitting half on, half off Dash's lap.

'I still can't work out what Finch was doing,' Polo said.

'And we can't believe you've gone on about it all day!' laughed Bobby.

The bus crunched over a hole in the road.

'That's the fun bus just asking for a song!' Legin called out. 'Don't worry 'bout the words, don't matter if they're wrong!'

'He's off again,' Tink laughed. 'Always speaking in rhymes.'

'Get your voices singing, get the tune a-ringing!'

Legin continued. 'Let's get this old bus jumping!
'Cos my tunes are heavy pumping!'

The back row burst into song and it felt to Bobby
like the bus started to speed up. Telegraph poles
whizzed past his window. Birds scattered into the air
from bushes and trees as the bus rumbled past,
pushed on by the singing inside.

The bus turned a sharp corner then started to slow
as the road began to rise steeply.

'Reggae is what reggae does!' Legin roared,
shifting down through the gears. 'Now sing out
loud to move our bus!'

The fun bus shook and an angry hissing sound cut through the air.

'Here we go again!' said Doug. 'Spook Hill!'

The bus was climbing steeply now.

'Why is it called Spook Hill?' Bobby asked.

'Because it's well spooky, that's why!' Polo said.

'I love it!' said Tink.

'Yeah, but you're weird,' said Dash.

Bobby stared through the window as the bus slowed to a crawl. Spook Hill was dark. Trees hung over the road, their branches reaching out like thin fingers. He saw the black shapes of crows take to the air.

The bus heaved a huge sigh of relief as it made it to the top of Spook Hill. Then Bobby saw a house slowly appear behind the trees.

'That place looks like something out of a horror movie!' whispered Polo. 'Imagine living there!'

The house was a lonely place, Bobby thought. Its grey bricks hidden in shadow, the path to the front door a thin line of broken stone. The lawn was overgrown. It was a place without colour. Cold.

'Does anyone live there?' Bobby asked.

Tiles were missing from the roof. Windows were broken. It looked abandoned, he thought.

'Yeah, your best friend from this morning,' said Dash. 'You know, bald, thin, grey overalls?'

'Mr Finch?' blurted Bobby. 'No way!'

'Yes way!' replied the gang.

'Lives there on his own,' Doug said. 'And it's haunted, you know.'

Bobby stared at the house as the bus rolled past. 'Haunted? You're pulling my leg!'

Doug shook his head. 'My dad saw it.'

'What?'

'The Lady in White,' Tink said.

Bobby was about to speak when something caught his eye. 'What's that?' he asked, pointing at the house.

The rest of the gang snapped their eyes around to where Bobby was pointing. And there, in a window in the highest point of the house, was the faint silhouette of someone watching them.

The bus left the house behind.

'Did you see that?' asked Tink. 'Please tell me you all saw it!'

'It didn't look like Finch,' Bobby said, a chill creeping across his skin.

'And if it wasn't Finch,' Polo said, 'then who was it?'

'Exactly,' said Doug.

As the bus drove away from Spook Hill, Bobby and his friends fell quiet. Whatever they had all seen, they were none of them keen to talk about it. But that didn't stop Bobby's inquisitive mind playing it over and over again as he headed on home.

That night, Bobby was lying in bed. Ruffian was snoring at the bottom of the bed, happy in his dreams. Bobby, though, was wide awake.

'There is something weird about that house,' he thought. 'Who was that in the window if it wasn't Mr Finch?'

Bobby started to hum the song his mum had taught him to sing when he was scared. Not that he was scared now, just intrigued. What had he seen?

The hum made way for words his mum had taught him, and Bobby sang, 'May each day be filled with blessings, like the sun that always lights the sky. May you always have great courage to spread your wings and fly.'

And then it happened again! First Bobby felt a

tingle in his toes, then a shiver raced up his spine, and finally a very bright light seemed to explode out of nowhere.

Flutes and songbirds and the sound of running water next, Bobby thought. Then, far off, he spotted a blob of bright swirling colours. Soon, he was picking up speed, rushing towards it, faster and faster! Then his ears popped and he heard a deafening, high-pitched 'zip' sound. Then silence. He was no longer moving.

Bobby opened his eyes, wondering just what kind of adventure he had landed in this time. Then he immediately wished he hadn't, because he was now standing outside the creepy house on top of Spook Hill.

7

The House on Spook Hill

Bobby watched as the front door of Spook House opened slowly, the hinges squealing painfully. He shifted nervously as a gust of wind made some chimes by the front door sing a tuneless melody, every note battling to be heard above the other.

From the darkness behind the door the pale face of a boy peered out from underneath neatly combed black hair, his tiny hands clasped together at his waist. He was wearing shiny black shoes, with heavy woollen socks pulled up to his knees where they met the top of a pair of grey tweed shorts.

'Who are you?' he asked, his voice as soft as Ruffian's blanket when it's been freshly washed and hung to dry in the summer sun. 'Why are you here? I've never seen you before.'

'I don't really know why I'm here, to be honest,' said Bobby.

'No one comes here, not ever!' said the small boy. 'You should go!'

'Why?' Bobby asked. 'Is something wrong?'

The boy said nothing and just stared back at Bobby.

Bobby didn't move. 'What's your name?' he asked.

'Harold,' the boy said. 'But you must go. You really must. It's for the best.'

That's an old name, Bobby thought, and held out a hand. 'I'm Bobby. Pleased to meet you!'

For a moment the boy hesitated, then he reached out and shook Bobby's hand. The chimes rang again, breaking the brief silence between the boys.

'I love your house!' Bobby said, noticing now how it looked different to when he had seen it from the school bus. Then, it had looked old and tired. Now, the paint seemed bright and new, no windows were broken, and the lawn was as perfect as a village bowling green.

'Really?' said Harold, his eyes staring at the floor.

'It doesn't look haunted at all!'

'Haunted?' Harold said. 'What are you talking about?'

'Oh, er, nothing,' Bobby said.

For a moment neither Bobby nor Harold moved or spoke. Then, just as Bobby thought Harold was about to close the door, the boy whispered, 'Do you want to come in?'

Jumping at the chance to see inside the Spook Hill house, Bobby stepped through the door. Harold closed it behind them.

Bobby shivered in the cold gloom inside the house as his eyes tried to adjust to the darkness.

'Sorry it's so chilly,' Harold said. 'Dad doesn't light fires. Not anymore.'

The inside of the house was as decayed as the outside had looked from the school bus. A stale smell lingered in the air. Dozens of black and white photos, in ornate wooden frames, hung on dark-red papered walls. Beneath them were old lamps with dusty shades.

Bobby noticed that the photos were of Harold with his mum and dad. In some, he was just a baby,

in others a little younger than he was now. An imposing wooden staircase swept its way upstairs in front of him.

A beam of sunlight streamed into the room through heavy brown curtains, cutting through the sombre gloom. In a far corner Bobby noticed a huge piano, white with dust.

'Do you play?' Bobby asked, nodding over at the grand piano.

'No one plays, not anymore,' Harold replied, looking down at his shoes. 'Not even at Christmas. And we used to, you know? All of us, around the piano, singing carols together. It was really special.'

Harold's voice faded and Bobby wondered then why there was no music in the house. And to have no carols at Christmas, well, something terrible must have happened, but what? And how could he help?

Harold interrupted Bobby's thoughts and asked, 'Do you want to see my room?'

'Yes please,' Bobby said, and followed Harold towards the stairs. He stared up at the photos hung on the wall. 'Are all your photos in black and white?' Bobby asked, pointing to one of Harold sitting with his mum and dad in a meadow.

'Why wouldn't they be?' Harold asked, and led the way up the stairs, then along a corridor thick with shadow.

'This is my room,' Harold said, pushing open a door at the far end of the hall.

'Got any cool computer games?' Bobby asked, following Harold inside.

'What's a computer?' asked Harold.

Bobby laughed, then saw the room. There was no computer. He couldn't see any toys either. Just a bed and a brown chest of drawers. In the corner of the room, Bobby saw that something was hidden underneath a large sheet.

'What's that?' Bobby asked.

Harold walked over and tugged at the sheet. It fell to the floor to reveal a rocking horse.

'It was a Christmas present,' Harold said, but his voice was sad. 'I've got this as well.'

Harold went to his bed and from underneath it pulled out a wooden box.

'What is it?' Bobby asked.

Harold opened the box. 'My toy train,' he said.

It, like the rocking horse, was made of wood, Bobby noticed. 'My grandad had one just like that when he was young,' he said.

It was then that Bobby began to wonder something. First, there was the fact that the house looked so different outside from when he had last seen it. Then, there were all the black and white photos. And finally, there was Harold's room, with no computer and with wooden toys.

'Harold,' Bobby said, 'can I ask you a really, really strange question?'

'I suppose so,' Harold said, walking over to the chest of drawers.

'What year is it?' Bobby asked.

Harold looked confused. 'It's 1947,' he said, and pulled out a picture from one of the drawers. 'When else would it be? This is Mum, by the way,' he said. 'Nothing has been the same since she died.'

Bobby didn't know what to say so instead he just

put his arm around Harold. 'That's really sad,' he said. Harold placed the photo away. Bobby knew that he needed to do something to cheer Harold up. 'Have you ever made a den?' he asked.

Harold gave a half-smile. 'Once,' he said. 'A long time ago.'

'Then let's make another!' Bobby said. 'To the garden!'

As Harold and Bobby turned to leave, the sound of heavy footsteps slipped into the room from somewhere deep inside the house.

'You have to go!' Harold said.

'Why?' asked Bobby. 'What's going on? Is something wrong?'

Harold grabbed Bobby by the arm and pulled him towards his bedroom door.

'Please!' Harold said. 'Hurry!'

'But why?' Bobby asked. Then he remembered what his friends had said about the house being haunted. Was it true? Is that why Harold was so scared?

'Is it the Lady in White?' Bobby asked.

Harold looked at Bobby, confusion in the lines creasing his face. From outside the room, the sound of footsteps was growing louder.

'There's no White Lady!' Harold said, pushing Bobby out of his bedroom and into the hallway. 'It's just me and Dad. Nothing has been the same since we lost Mum. Dad is so unhappy and so sad. I always try to make sure that nothing bothers him. And I don't want you to get into trouble!'

Bobby stopped in his tracks. From the far end of the corridor, he saw a huge shadow stretching slowly towards them, getting closer and closer.

8

The Lady in White

Bobby could hear the footsteps getting louder as the shadow grew, the tick-tock of the grandfather clock in the hall marking the rhythm of each step.

Bobby was about to place himself between Harold and the approaching shadow. But when he glanced at Harold, he saw that the boy wasn't scared at all, just sad.

'It's alright,' Harold said, and put a hand on Bobby's arm. Then he turned to the shadow and said, 'Hello, Father.'

The shadow moved closer and from the gloom a

frail man emerged, his face riven with lines of sorrow.

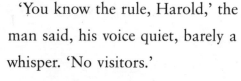

'You know the rule, Harold,' the man said, his voice quiet, barely a whisper. 'No visitors.'

The man sounded so sad, Bobby thought, like something inside him was broken beyond repair.

'We don't open the door to anyone, Son, remember?'

Harold turned his eyes down to the floor.

'You do remember why, don't you?'

'Yes, Father,' Harold answered.

'Good, then show your guest to the door, and we'll not talk of this again.'

Harold's dad continued along the corridor, fading back into the darkness and shadows.

Bobby let out a deep sigh. 'I've never seen or heard someone so sad,' he said.

'I think a piece of him died with Mum,' Harold said, as he started to walk down the staircase. 'I miss her, but I miss him, too, you know. He had such a wonderful laugh!'

Bobby chased after Harold, bumping into him on the bottom step. 'Why no visitors?' he asked.

'It's hard to explain,' Harold said. 'But you must go now, I don't want to upset Dad.'

Harold ushered Bobby towards the front door.

Bobby stopped dead, refusing to go any further. 'Listen, Harold, I want to help. But you have to be honest with me. I know you said that there isn't a ghost, but—'

'There's no ghost!' Harold said, cutting Bobby's voice in two.

Bobby said nothing, waiting to see if Harold was going to say any more.

At last, Harold spoke again.

'Dad hasn't wanted anyone here since Mum died,' he explained. 'He misses her voice, the way she used to play the piano, and doesn't want to hear anyone else where she used to be. He thinks that it would be just too painful, to hear happiness in this house again. Even at Christmas.'

Bobby looked at the dusty piano in the corner.

'She would sit and play,' Harold said. 'She and Dad would sing. No one has sung in this house since. We don't even hum or whistle anymore.'

'Not even carols at Christmas,' Bobby said, remembering what Harold had said earlier.

'No, not even that,' Harold said, shaking his head. Then he took a very deep breath and turned and walked slowly towards the front door.

Bobby was about to move, but something stopped him. He tried again, but as he stepped forward he found that instead of walking towards the door, he was walking towards the piano! He tried to stop himself but couldn't. What on earth was going on?

'Er, Harold?' Bobby said, as the piano drew closer.

'What are you doing?' Harold asked, staring at Bobby. 'You need to leave! Please!'

'I'm not doing anything!' Bobby said, trying to turn towards the door. 'I'm really not! It's my legs, not me! They're just walking, like they've a mind of their own! Help!'

Bobby tried to stop himself walking. But his legs just kept moving. It was like someone else was in control of his body! He was helpless. And then he was at the piano and sitting down.

'Please, don't touch it!' Harold said, dashing over. 'You can't! Father said! It'll make him even more sad, and I need to look after him and make sure that doesn't happen!'

'But I can't even play!' Bobby said, as his hands reached out for the keys.

Notes filled the air, then, like beautiful musical butterflies. Bobby's fingers danced up and down the piano keys.

'Please, you have to stop,' Harold said, rushing over to Bobby. 'Please!'

Bobby opened his mouth to answer, but instead he started to sing. His voice spiralled through the house, twisting and turning and dancing in the dust and the darkness. The tune was alive and soaring, a spirit trapped in a box, finally released.

Bobby saw the panic on Harold's face, as the music filled the air, but there was nothing he could do to stop. Something, or someONE, was in control of what he was doing.

A thunderous crack split the air and the house shuddered to the sound of a door crashing open upstairs.

'It's Dad!' Harold said. 'Bobby! Please stop. Please! He'll be so upset and I can't bear to see him cry, not anymore!'

Then Harold's dad was striding down the stairs towards them.

Bobby tried to pull his hands off the piano keys but they were stuck there. He tried again, but his fingers just kept on playing. Then, in the middle of the room, a warm light broke through the shadows, but it was not of the sun. To Bobby, it was as though the light was a living thing, and it was moving in time to his music and song.

'Look, Father!' said Harold, as the room became ablaze with light. 'The dust is dancing!'

And true enough, the light had breathed life into the stale dust and, in the sunbeams, it swirled around the room, rejoicing in time to the music.

Harold spun around to his dad, his excitement knocking him off balance. 'Father! Can you smell that? The room. It . . . it smells like Mother!'

Harold's dad stood at the bottom of the stairs, his mouth open, his eyes wide. 'It's jasmine,' he said, walking towards Bobby at the piano. 'It was her perfume!'

'Don't stop playing, Bobby. Please don't stop,' Harold said. 'It's Mum! It has to be. She's here!'

Bobby couldn't stop, even if he wanted to! It was as if someone was sitting next to him on the piano stool pulling the song out of him.

Then, as Bobby continued to sing and play, Harold ran to his dad and they embraced each other in the fragrant, sun-filled room.

Harold's dad pulled himself away from his son, then walked round the piano to sit next to Bobby.

'Mind if we join in?'

Then Harold's dad was playing the piano, and both he and Harold were singing along.

At last, Bobby was suddenly back in control of his own body and he stopped playing, stepping away from the piano as Harold sat down next to his father.

The light in the room was growing, sunlight and dust twisting in a tornado, pulling itself into the faint image of a woman, a faded photo brought to life. And from out of the sun-drenched dust came the sound of another voice, high and honeyed.

'It's the Lady in White!' Bobby said, as the faint image grew stronger with every note.

'Hello, love!' Harold's dad said, as Bobby watched the woman, who was now in the room with them all, glide over towards the piano.

Harold's dad looked over to Bobby. 'Sing with us?' he asked, his voice soft and full of emotion.

And so, the family launched into song, the closeness reminding Bobby of the photos he'd seen in the hallway.

'I'm so glad you've let the music back in!' said

Harold's mum, holding close her husband and son. 'Now, you must let the light back into this house and into your hearts. I'll be with you forever, but you must let me go!'

Bobby looked over to the piano, and both father and son were smiling and laughing and hugging, their cheeks streaming with tears, not of sadness but happiness. And with that, he saw the ghostly image of Harold's mum, smiling with her family, and fading into the bright, heavenly light.

Then, as Harold and his dad sung on, Bobby felt a familiar sensation in his toes, a gentle tingle, creeping upwards.

9

Mr Finch Saves the Day

A shiver raced up Bobby's spine and then he
heard a sound he recognised, a very high-
pitched 'zip'. And off he went, once again spinning
through the blob of bright swirling colours. Where
once the whirling had made him feel a bit sick, now
Bobby was loving it! He was weightless, rolling and
back flipping through the dark without a care, his
hair catching in the wind, like he was on a

rollercoaster. Distant stars were flashing, then came the sounds of flutes and songbirds and running water.

Bobby closed his eyes. And then there was silence.

For a moment, Bobby didn't move. Then he noticed a faint scent of flowers in the air. It was jasmine, and he knew it well, as it was the smell of his own mum's perfume.

Opening his eyes, Bobby breathed a sigh of relief. He was back on the farm and in his own bed.

Bobby heard another sound and saw at the bottom of his bed the furry lump of Ruffian, fast asleep, and snoring. He reached out and stroked Ruffian's huge tired head. The dog let out a soft, gentle rumble of a growl that was almost a cat's purr.

Lying back on his pillow, Bobby closed his eyes, his mind drifting back to what had happened at the house on Spook Hill. It had been a little bit scary, yes, but in the end, it was as though the house had woken up from a terrible dream. Harold and his dad were happy now, Bobby thought, and that was good, and the Lady in White was a memory who would no longer haunt them, but dance and sing and play with them forever more.

And with happy thoughts of his adventure, Bobby drifted off to the land of nod.

After another huge breakfast, this time of boiled eggs, toast soldiers and the best smoothie ever, Bobby was back on the bus with his friends and heading for school. Legin was on good form and singing and rapping his every word.

'With no forewarning, it's another school morning!' Legin sang, writing new words to the tune spinning its way out of the old stereo. 'And it is pouring, but we ain't boring! Ain't that right, kids? 'Cos we're a-storming!'

Everyone on the fun bus cheered.

'Next stop Spook Hill!' Legin shouted.

The children on the bus turned to squash their faces against the bus windows as the creepy house came up to greet them.

'Hey look!' shouted Dash. 'Isn't that old Finch outside his house?'

'It can't be,' said Tink, 'he's smiling!'

And sure enough, as the bus drove alongside the

house, Bobby saw that Mr Finch was standing outside the front door smiling, and waving energetically at the bus!

'I told you he wasn't all that bad,' Bobby said.

'Well, he certainly looks happy,' Polo shrugged. 'Wonder what that's all about then?'

As the bus rumbled on, Bobby thought back to what had happened the night before, when he had visited Harold. The house was definitely a happier place, he thought, glancing back at Finch. But why was the caretaker so happy now?

Bobby shook his head, trying to get his thoughts into order. Then ahead, the school gates came into view and Legin beeped his horn.

Later that day, Bobby was in the school hall with the rest of the cast for the school nativity.

'Bobby!' Miss Evans called over to him. 'You're up! Give it all you got!'

Tink pushed 'play' on the music system and hit the lights, and the spotlight fell on Bobby, who was centre stage. He started to sing.

'Once in royal David's city, stood a lowly cattle shed . . .'

BANG!

'Not again!' Miss Evans sighed, the hall once again in darkness. 'Katinka, can you fix those lights, please?'

'Think so, Miss!' Tink shouted back over the music.

'Keep singing, Bobby!' Miss Evans said.

Bobby took a deep breath, ready for the second verse.

'He came down to earth from heaven . . .'

The music stopped.

'Miss, the sound system's gone now!' Tink cried. 'Give me a minute to fix it.'

Bobby was standing with the rest of the cast in dark silence when Polo called out. 'Miss Evans!'

'Yes?'

'I think there's someone on stage with us again!'

'Oh, don't be so silly,' Miss Evans said.

'No, he's right,' said Dash. 'I think I heard footsteps.'

'Me too!' added Doug. 'And a weird rumbling sound. What is it?'

'No idea,' Bobby said, trying to see in the dark.

The hall burst into light as Tink fixed the lights,

119

and there, standing next to Bobby, was Mr Finch. At his side was the school piano.

'Thank you, Mr Finch,' Miss Evans said. 'That's very kind of you but, unfortunately, no one here plays the piano, and I'm very sure it's terribly out of tune. Katinka, can you fix the sound system, please?'

'Don't think so, Miss, the file's corrupted!' Tink replied.

Mr Finch smiled at Bobby and reached for the music sheets he was holding. Bobby handed them over and watched the caretaker sit down at the piano.

'From the top, eh Bobby?' Mr Finch said with a wink. 'We should LET THE MUSIC BACK into this hall, don't you think?'

And it was then that Bobby realised who Mr Finch was.

'Harold?'

Mr Finch nodded and smiled.

'I don't really know what happened, Bobby,' he said. 'But something did, didn't it? It's like a very distant memory, a dream perhaps.'

'It wasn't a dream,' Bobby smiled.

'All my bad memories, they're gone,' Mr Finch said. 'I don't really understand it. Do you?'

Bobby smiled and shrugged his shoulders. 'I think,' he said, 'it's just that music is a little bit magic, if you believe in it enough.'

'And I do!' Mr Finch said, and started to play.

10

Secret Santa and the Missing Presents

'What type of key do you need for a nativity?' Polo asked. 'Anyone? Any ideas?'

Bobby and his friends were in the school hall enjoying lunch on the final day of term, which was all decorated for Christmas, including a huge tree beneath which were piled masses of Secret Santa presents. Bobby still hadn't put his own present under the tree, because he wasn't so sure it was all that good. It was a song he had written all by himself.

'Look at all those presents!' Tink said. 'Can't wait to get mine!'

'Yeah, neither can I,' Bobby said. 'I've never done Secret Santa before.'

'I'm trying to tell a joke here,' Polo said.

'It was Mr Morris's idea,' Tink explained. 'It's a totally fab way of making sure everyone at school gives and receives a present, don't you think? For a head teacher, he's not bad, really, is he?'

Polo stood up, clearly not giving up on his joke. 'Drumroll, please!' he said. 'A don-key! Ha!'

Bobby groaned at the joke, not least because he couldn't really remember how it had begun, and went back to finishing off his food. It was Christmas dinner, his favourite, with turkey and all the trimmings, including the crunchiest, most delicious roast potatoes ever. They weren't quite as good as his mum's, Bobby thought, but they were close. Polo had finished his meal first and was now trying to keep them entertained, while scraping up the last few crumbs of roast potatoes from his plate. Everyone was wearing party hats from the crackers they had all pulled.

'Your jokes are worse than Mr Morris's,' Bobby said.

'My jokes are wondrous!' Mr Morris bellowed, appearing suddenly at the end of their table, and dressed like Santa Claus.

'Here we go again,' Tink said, rolling her eyes, but a smile lighting up her face.

'So, who's Santa's favourite singer?' Mr Morris asked, his enormous moustache wiggling excitedly.

No one answered, everyone instead looking awkwardly at their nearly empty plates.

'Elf-is Presley!' Mr Morris announced. 'Comedy gold, am I right? Honestly, I should be on stage in front of the Queen, I'm so funny!'

'Good one, sir!' said Bobby, as Mr Morris walked off as proud as a peacock.

'Shall we run through our lines one more time?' asked Dash. 'The nativity is only a couple of hours away now. And I don't want Mary giving birth at the wrong time!'

Before anyone had a chance to run through their lines, Wayne, the school bully, walked past the table and flicked Bobby's party hat into his gravy.

'Wayne! Pack it in, will you!' said Tink. 'It's Christmas!'

Wayne ignored her and proceeded to knock

everyone's party hats off their heads, before walking away, laughing to himself.

'He only gets away with it because his mum's the cook!' said Doug.

Bobby watched Wayne go, and noticed that he gave his mum, Mrs Crouch, a nod, before he left the hall.

'Good riddance to the bully!' remarked Dash.

'Quiet, you noisy rabble!'

Everyone jumped. Bobby looked up to see Mrs Crouch standing over them, a grey whisker on her chin flicking at him.

'Plates to the end of the table so I can clear, ready for dessert. NOW!'

As Mrs Crouch walked off, Dash leant across the table and stared at Bobby. 'Her food's good, but she's properly horrible,' she said. 'She once set fire to all the wooden spoons so that dessert couldn't be served!'

'No way!' Bobby said.

'It's true,' said Tink. 'And if she doesn't like you, she'll put chilli powder in your food.'

Just then the lights flickered, and the canteen was plunged into darkness.

'Have you broken the school lights again, Tink?' Doug said.

Everyone laughed then Polo started to make ghost sounds.

Finally, after five minutes or so, during which there had been a lot of screaming as Polo continued with his spooky sound effects, the lights came back on.

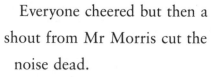

Everyone cheered but then a shout from Mr Morris cut the noise dead.

Bobby looked over to where Mr Morris was standing, next to the Christmas tree, and saw immediately that something was terribly wrong. And of all the terribly wrong things Bobby could imagine, this was by far the most terribly wrong thing ever.

'The presents!' Bobby said, pointing at the Christmas tree. 'They're gone!'

A shocked silence swept through the hall as everyone stared at where, just a moment ago, there had been a huge pile of presents.

'We have a thief among us!' shouted Mr Morris, his Scottish accent getting stronger and stronger. 'And unless we get the presents back, well, Christmas will be cancelled!'

Bobby could see that not only was Mr Morris angry and upset, but so was everyone else in in the hall. The Secret Santa presents were all gone, gifts everyone in the school had bought to share with everyone else. Bobby felt angry and upset, too, and before he could stop himself, he was singing again.

'Bobby?' Doug asked. 'You OK? I'm not sure now's the best time to be rehearsing, do you?'

But Bobby wasn't listening to Doug, because his toes were tingling and then a shiver raced up his spine.

Bobby knew exactly what was happening and, as Doug's voice faded, so did the hall and everyone in it. Then Bobby was off, spinning and cart-wheeling through the galaxy with bright-coloured planets whizzing by. Bobby, now very used to the magic that sometimes happened when he sang, lay on his back, with his arms behind his head, as he moved towards the blob of bright swirling colours, and another adventure.

11

Bobby Dean
Goes to Lapland

With his eyes firmly shut, Bobby could hear the pitter patter of what sounded like tiny footsteps running past him in every direction. There were voices, too, squeaky ones, and they were arguing. And behind all of this came the sound of rap music and the jingling of bells.

Bobby stood up and, opening his eyes, saw that

he was in an enormous room decorated in red, white and gold, with Christmas trees and presents everywhere. It went on for as far as the eye could see.

'Oi, what's the weather like up there?' said a high-pitched voice.

Bobby looked around but couldn't see anyone.

'Hey, giant chops!' said a voice that was almost a squeak.

Bobby looked around again, but still nothing. So, who on earth was speaking to him?

'Ouch!' Bobby said, as a sharp prod jabbed into his shin. He looked down and saw standing by his feet two very small people, about as tall as his knees, each with very large ears. One had very long blonde hair tied in plaits. The other had a very impressive, pointy beard.

'Er, hi,' Bobby said. 'I'm Bobby.'

'You're very big,' said the one with the pointy beard. 'Are all Bobbys big? Do you come from Big Bobby Land?'

'And you're very small,' Bobby replied, ignoring

the questions. He dropped to his knees. 'There, that's better!'

'We're elves,' said the one with the long blonde hair. 'I'm Sage. And this is my less good-looking brother, Onion.'

'Welcome to Lapland!' said Onion. 'I'm Onion! And this is Sage, my sister!'

Sage jabbed Onion in the ribs. 'I've just told him that!'

'Really?'

'Yes!'

'But I wanted to,' Onion said, and folded his arms then stomped a foot.

Bobby took another look around him. 'So, is this Santa's Grotto?' he asked.

Onion waved an arm to take in everything around them. 'Over there we have the mail room, next to it the painting room,' he said. 'Then it's the toy factory, and finally, the wrapping room. They love loud music and a rhyme in there!'

Sage looked back up at Bobby. 'You're here to help, yes?' she asked. 'With the terrible thing that's just happened?'

'What terrible thing?' Bobby asked.

'Ooh, it's very terrible,' Onion said. 'The most terrible thing ever! Can you feel how terrible it is? I can! It's squeezing me and I don't like it at all!'

Sage said, 'Big Daddy Bing, our chief elf, has run off. He's the only one who can keep this place running to schedule. Now, because he's gone, all the other elves have gone on strike.'

'He's got fed up with always giving presents away and never getting any,' Onion said.

'Do you know where he is?' Bobby asked.

Onion gave a sharp nod. 'He's gone to the Sno-Go caves on the edge of the—' Onion looked around as if to see whether anyone was listening in, then whispered, '—Disenchanted Forest. It's a scary place that no one should go to! And he's taken Santa's sleigh with him!'

'What happens if he doesn't come back?' Bobby asked.

'Christmas is cancelled,' said Sage.

'Looks like we need to save Christmas, then,' Bobby said. 'So, how do we get to the Disenchanted Forest?'

'I can help with that!' said a thunderous voice and Bobby turned around to see Santa Claus himself.

141

'So, Bobby Dean has come to save the day?' Santa said. 'And not a moment too soon! Follow me!'

Santa led Bobby, Sage and Onion to what Bobby thought looked a bit like a big slide at a swimming pool. It twisted and turned for what seemed like miles!

'This is the toy chute,' Santa said. 'It leads to the loading area. Your ride to the Disenchanted Forest will meet you at the bottom.'

Then, before Bobby could do anything about it, Santa picked him up and plopped him into the chute. And he was off!

Bobby sped down the chute, twisting left and right, going faster and faster.

'This is amazing!' Bobby yelled, and a moment

later he shot out of the bottom of the chute and rolled head over heels onto a huge soft mattress.

'Hello, Bobby!'

Bobby looked up to find himself face to face with a snowman wearing a very posh hat and shiny gloves.

'I'm Frosterson von Carrotnose, your driver,' the snowman said. 'But you can call me Frosty!'

'But you don't have a car,' Bobby said, looking around as he climbed to his feet.

'No, but I do have this,' Frosterson said, and

pointed at a strange machine close by. 'This is my snowmobile. Like it?'

The machine had a pair of skis at the front for steering, and caterpillar tracks at the back to power it through the snow. The seats were covered in thick fur.

Frosty lifted Bobby onto the snowmobile then climbed on himself.

'Hold on, Bobby!'

Bobby reached his arms around the snowman and then they were off!

The snowmobile roared as they raced through the snow, throwing out great clouds of white behind them as they went. Bobby looked behind to see Santa's Grotto growing smaller and smaller, until finally he couldn't see it at all. High above, the bright moon made the snow shine and glisten, as though covered in a carpet of the tiniest diamonds. And the air tingled when Bobby breathed it in, almost as though he was sucking in sherbet!

They passed frozen lakes and dense pine forests. Frosty pointed out to Bobby the Northern Lights which danced high above them, their colours of green, pink, red, violet and white all twisting and turning between Bobby and stars far beyond.

A few minutes later, Bobby noticed that the snowmobile was slowing.

'We're nearly there,' Frosty said. 'You ready to save Christmas, Bobby?'

'You bet I am!' Bobby said, and saw, just ahead of them, the opening of a cave and, beyond it, the quiet darkness of the Disenchanted Forest.

12

Bobby Dean Saves Christmas

As Bobby and Frosty, the snowman, approached the edge of the Disenchanted Forest in the snowmobile, they saw Big Daddy Bing, the chief elf, sitting outside one of the Sno-Go Caves.

'Go do your thing, Bobby,' said Frosty. 'And good luck!'

Bobby climbed off the snowmobile when something slipped from his pocket and down onto the snow. It was his Secret Santa present. And seeing it gave him an idea.

Bobby walked over to Bing, smiling his biggest smile, but the elf just ignored him.

'Hello, Big Daddy Bing,' Bobby said. 'My name's Bobby Dean. It's great to meet you!'

'No, it isn't,' Bing replied. 'It's rubbish. Go away. Leave me alone.'

'I can't do that,' Bobby said.

'Why not?' Bing asked. 'I don't know who you are or why you're here. I just want to be left alone! So, poo to you and to whoever sent you. Yes, you heard me: poo to you!'

'But if I go, then I can't give you this,' Bobby said, ignoring Bing's grump, and he held out the envelope containing his very special song.

'And what's that?' Bing asked.

'It's a present,' Bobby said. 'Just for you.'

Bing stared at Bobby. 'I bet it isn't,' he said. 'I bet it's an exploding pie or a huge spider or just a rock.'

'It's none of those things,' Bobby said. 'It really is a present.'

'And it's for me?' Bing asked.

'Of course,' Bobby said.

'But who's it from?'

'Now that would be telling,' Bobby said. 'It's a Secret Santa present, so whoever wanted you to have it has decided to keep it a secret.'

'No one's ever given me a present,' Bing said. 'Not ever, not even just once.'

'Well, they have now,' said Bobby, buttering up the chief elf with kindness. 'Why don't you open it and see what it is?'

Big Daddy Bing reached out and took the envelope, then opened it. 'It's a song,' he said.

'Really?' Bobby said, doing his best to sound surprised. 'Well, if someone wrote you a song, then they must think you are very special indeed. How amazing is that?'

'Do you think so?' Bing asked. 'No one else does. That's why I'm here.'

'They do, you know,' Bobby said. 'Santa himself said that he can't do Christmas without your help. That's how special you are. That's how important.'

Big Daddy Bing stared at the song. 'I'm not very good at singing,' he said. 'And I can't actually read music.'

'Well, it just so happens that I can,' said Bobby. 'So, why don't we learn it together on the way back to Santa's workshop?'

The journey back to Lapland was even more tuneful than being on Legin's bus on the way to school. Frosty joined in as Bobby helped Bing to learn his song.

'You have a fantastic voice!' Bobby said.

'It's true, you do!' Frosty agreed.

When they arrived back at the workshop, Santa and all of the elves were there to greet them.

'Well done, Bobby!' Santa bellowed, his big furry face a huge warm smile. 'And welcome back, Big Daddy Bing!'

Bing jumped off the snowmobile. 'Look!' he said, holding out Bobby's song. 'Someone gave me a Secret Santa present!'

'Secret Santa, hey?' Santa said, winking at

Bobby. 'Well, that sounds like just the kind of thing we should have here, wouldn't you agree, Bing?'

'Very much so, yes,' Bing said, 'but before that, I think we need to do something else.'

'And what's that?' Santa asked.

Big Daddy Bing smiled wide. 'We've a Christmas deadline to keep!' he bellowed. 'Back to work, everyone! Let's do this!'

As the elves busied themselves preparing all the presents for the big day, Santa took Bobby to one side.

'You were already on the "good" list, Bobby, but now you're at the very top! Thank you! You've saved Christmas!'

'Happy to help,' Bobby said.

Santa then bent down, picked up a mound of snow and crushed it into the most perfect snowball.

'Now there's another little job for you,' Santa said, and breathed on the snowball, turning it into ice as clear as glass. 'Look!'

Bobby peered into the ice ball and saw Wayne and his mum with the Secret Santa presents from school.

Bobby couldn't believe what he was seeing.

'Keep watching!' Santa said.

The scene changed to a care home, and Bobby watched as Wayne and his mum handed out the presents they had taken from the school to the old people who lived there.

'So, they took the presents to give to people who

had nothing,' Bobby said. 'I need to get back and sort things out!'

A moment later, Bobby felt a tingle through his body.

'See you around, Bobby!' Santa said.

'Thanks for your help!' said Sage and Onion.

'You rock!' Bing shouted, fist pumping the air.

Then Bobby was zipping through the blob of swirling colours once again.

The next thing Bobby knew, he was back in the school canteen the following day. Mr Morris, his face still red with rage, was standing by the Christmas tree. Wayne and Mrs Crouch were in front of him, their heads bowed.

'I've found the thieves!' Mr Morris declared.

'No! You haven't, sir!' shouted Bobby.

'But I know they did it!' Mr Morris said, staring

at Bobby. 'They had all of the presents because they had taken them in rather a naughty fashion, I must say. And that really isn't what Christmas is about, is it? No, no it isn't! These are two very naughty people indeed!'

'You're right, they did take them,' Bobby said. 'But there's more to it, I promise you.'

'Nonsense!' Mr Morris huffed. 'I found them being very naughty and I don't really see how there is anything more to say on the matter!'

'They did it to make other people happy!' Bobby said, his words blurting out before he could stop himself.

'I beg your pardon?' Mr Morris said. 'They took the presents to make people happy? But that doesn't make any sense, Bobby, because we were all very, very sad!'

Bobby looked over to Wayne. 'I'm right, aren't I?' Bobby said. 'Tell Mr Morris! Tell him why you took the Secret Santa presents!'

Wayne stared at Bobby, his eyes wide with confusion.

'Tell everyone about the care home,' Bobby said. 'Please!'

'Tell me what about where now?' Mr Morris asked.

'It's, well, there's this care home,' Wayne said at last. 'My grandma is there, too, you see. They don't have much. And some of them don't get anything for Christmas at all. And, well, we just thought . . .'

'You just thought you could take our presents and give them away, did you?' Mr Morris asked. 'Is that it? Well, is it?'

'I know it was wrong,' Wayne said. 'And don't blame Mum, because it was my idea. It's just that, well, we've all got so much, haven't we? And they haven't. That's all. I'm sorry.'

Mr Morris clapped his hands to get everyone's attention.

'Well then,' he said, 'first, I think I must say that it really isn't a good idea to steal. That really was very, very naughty indeed!'

Bobby started to feel nervous. Was Mr Morris really going to punish Wayne and his mum?

'However,' Mr Morris said, 'you do have a point, Wayne. We do indeed have more than enough. So, can I ask, did the presents bring smiles to the faces of the people who received them?'

'Yes,' Wayne nodded. 'I've never seen them so happy.'

'Then I have an idea,' Mr Morris said, and turned to speak to the school. 'From this day forward, instead of Secret Santa, what say the school gives presents to people in our village who really need them? We would be following Wayne's example, and making people happy. Though without the naughty stealing, obviously, because that is both naughty and stealing,

so no more of that, thank you very much!'

The school hall erupted into cheers.

'Nice one, Bobby!' said Tink.

'I didn't do anything,' Bobby said.

'Yes, you did,' said another voice, and Bobby turned to see Wayne standing in front of him.

'Hi, Wayne,' Bobby said. 'I didn't agree with the stealing bit, but the giving presents away thing? That was cool.'

'Thanks,' Wayne said. 'We couldn't afford to give

everyone a present and we didn't really think about what we were doing. Thanks for sorting it all out.'

'Yeah, it was really cool actually,' said Doug.

'No stealing again, though, right?' Bobby said.

'Right,' agreed Wayne.

A shout from the front of the hall caught everyone's attention.

'Right, everyone!' Miss Evans said. 'There has been a change of plan to this afternoon. Instead of lessons, we're going to do something very special indeed. We are going to perform the nativity for Wayne's grandma and all of her friends at the home!'

The hall erupted into cheers and applause.

'You're alright, you know,' Wayne said to Bobby.

'You too, actually,' Bobby said.

And with that, everyone followed Miss Evans out of the hall, ready to give the performance of a lifetime.

13

In the Trenches

Bobby woke with a start. He checked his watch. Half past midnight? That meant it was Christmas Day! So, what had woken him up?

'Ruff?'

A snore from the end of his bed was the only answer Bobby got from his dog. So, if it hadn't been Ruff, then what?

Bobby wondered for a moment if it was Santa, remembering his adventures in Lapland. But then he heard a sound, a sharp crack, from downstairs.

Ruffian growled.

'You heard it too, right, Ruff?' said Bobby. 'Come on, let's go and see what it is.'

Bobby and Ruffian crept downstairs. Bobby heard the sound again, only there were other sounds, too, loud thumps and crashes and bangs.

Bobby pushed open the living room door. The room was vibrating with a deafening creak, crash and clunk. The television was on and someone was sitting in an armchair.

'Look, Ruff, it's Grumps!' Bobby said. 'He's fast asleep and snoring!'

Bobby's grandparents, Grumps and Gran, had come to spend Christmas with them.

Bobby turned to switch off the television and saw that Grumps had been watching one of his war films. It looked terrifying, Bobby thought. All that noise and shouting. Just seeing it made him sad and to cheer himself up he started to sing.

Bobby felt his stomach flip and once again he was spinning and whirling, as his whole body was tingling from head to foot. Then he was hurtling through the galaxy, tiny planets scurrying and whizzing by as if late for an important meeting, until at last he sped through a blob of colours, there was a loud 'zip' sound, and he was swallowed up into another time and another place.

Bobby opened his eyes to find himself in a muddy trench. The earth was shaking with booms, bangs and explosions. The air sung with shouts of soldiers and the roar and clatter of gunfire. He took in a nervous breath and could taste gunpowder in the air. There was a smell of mud and wet wood.

Bobby then noticed that he was

dressed like a soldier, in heavy
green trousers and jacket.

He had a tin helmet on his
head and big brown heavy
boots on his feet. He saw
other soldiers close by,
huddled together to keep
warm, steam rising from them
in the cold.

'Where am I now?' Bobby said
to himself.

'Dead Man's Trench,' a voice
replied.

Bobby saw a young soldier
sitting opposite.

'You're the new lad, right?' the soldier said. 'I'm
William Palmer. Bill for short.'

The soldier gave Bobby some bread and cheese in
a rusty tin which served as a plate.

Bobby nibbled the bread. It was damp and he
could taste the mould. The cheese smelt of
two-week-old socks.

169

'How old are you?' Bill asked.

'Nine,' Bobby said.

'And I thought I was the youngest!' Bill laughed.
'I'm 16, you see. Though I arrived when I was only
15. I lied about my age so I could do my bit for
Queen and country!'

A shout from another soldier bumped into Bill's
words.

'A mouse! There, by the new lad!'

Another soldier said, 'I saw it first, so I gets to
eat it!'

Everyone was up on their feet trying to catch the
mouse. Thinking quickly,
Bobby grabbed the mouse
and hid it in his pocket.

'Hey, where did it
go?' a soldier asked.

'Wasn't much meat on
it anyway,' said another.
Once the soldiers had
gone back to their
positions, Bobby

checked in on the mouse. To his surprise it was dressed like a soldier.

Then the mouse took off his tin hat, looked up at Bobby, and said, 'I'm Noel. Who are you?'

14

Noel Knows Best

Bobby and Bill watched as Noel, the mouse, tapped the dust off his clothes. Then he straightened his helmet and carefully placed his rifle over his shoulder.

Bobby introduced himself then said, 'And this is Bill. How long have you been down in the trenches?'

'Too long,' Noel said. 'This one for a few months, the German ones a few months before that.'

'But they're the enemy!' Bill said.

'They're not that different to you, you know?' said Noel.

'How do you mean?' Bobby asked.

'Well, if you went over the top, you'd see the German trenches just a few steps away from where we are now. And you know what? The soldiers there are scared and miles away from home. Just like everyone here.'

Bobby noticed that some of the other soldiers were listening in.

'Like everyone here, they're cold, hungry and missing their loved ones, too,' Noel said.

'I wonder what they're doing over there right now?' said Bobby.

A faint sound drifted over the top of the trench on a lonely gust of wind.

'Is that singing I can hear?' Bill asked.

Bobby was sure he recognised the tune, but the words were in German and he couldn't quite place it.

'It's *Silent Night*,' a soldier said.

Bobby listened in closely and, before he knew

what he was doing, he was singing along. As the German voices drifted through the air, Bobby found himself using their words, the foreign language coming to him as naturally as his own.

'Nice idea,' Noel said, nudging Bill, and they both joined in too in English.

Then, as the voices of Bobby, Bill and Noel rose to mingle with the words in the wind, other soldiers joined in, too.

When the carol came to an end, a voice called out from somewhere in the gloom.

'Happy Christmas, Tommies!' The accent was German, but the words were English.

'Who are the Tommies?' Bobby asked.

'We are,' Bill said. 'That's what they call us.'

A shout came from down the line. 'There's a white flag!'

'That means they want a truce,' Bill said. 'No shooting!'

Then, slowly, the soldiers started to peer over the top of the trench.

'What's happening?' Bobby asked.

Noel scurried up to the top of the trench. 'It's the Germans,' he said. 'They're waving to us and calling us over!'

'But isn't this a war?' Bobby asked.

Noel scurried back down to Bobby. 'I think they want to meet us.'

'Go out into No Man's Land?' Bill said. 'That's madness!'

'They're not armed,' Noel said, and looked at Bobby. 'What do you say, Bobby? Ready to be brave?'

Bobby was terrified but something deep down told him what he had to do. And before Bill could stop him, he climbed a ladder, and with Noel on his shoulder clinging on to his ear, went out to meet the enemy.

'Well, what are we waiting for?' shouted Bill, as the British soldiers climbed out of their trenches one by one.

'Look at that!' said Bobby, drawing Noel's attention to a sign the Germans were holding on which were the words, 'You not shoot, we not shoot'.

The ground between both trenches, which the soldiers called No Man's Land, was transformed. Sworn enemies were now exchanging gifts including chocolate, tins of beef and cigarettes.

'Please take this!' said a German soldier, handing Bobby a shiny button as if it was a piece of precious gold. 'Merry Christmas!' he said, and he gave Bobby a hug.

'Merry Christmas to you, too!' said Bobby, giving the German soldier the cheese he had in his pocket in return. The German soldier smiled through teary eyes. He looked no older than Bill.

Bobby noticed that more and more of the soldiers were hugging and shaking hands.

'This is the most amazing thing I've ever seen!' said Bobby to Noel.

'Certainly is!' said Noel, then he whispered into Bobby's ear, 'And I know just what we need now! How good are you at football?'

What followed was a football match between the German soldiers and the British, right there in No Man's Land, with Bobby in goal and Noel as the referee! Both sides were laughing and running around together.

Bobby stood there with his little friend perched on his shoulder, a warm feeling heating him inside.

'Wouldn't it be good if things could stay friendly and peaceful, like they are now, forever?' he said to Noel.

'I'm sorry to say, but this won't last!' answered Noel as he kept watch on the match.

'But at least now we've given both sides an idea of what peace will be like and how much better it is than war!'

The now familiar tingling sensation started creeping up Bobby's legs again. He shivered, nearly knocking Noel off his shoulder perch! And then Bobby was gone! Spat out through the high-pitched 'zip' and the blob of multicolours. And he was flying through

his own No Man's Land where the
stars and planets played their own
game of chase. Bobby hoped he
was going home for Christmas!

15

Santa Claus and the Magic Globe

Bobby opened his eyes to find himself back in his own living room.

'Oh! Bobby, that was beautiful!'

'Mum?'

Bobby shook his head to knock his eyes into focus and found that that he was standing in front of Grumps, Gran, Ruffian, and his mum and dad.

'You were singing *Silent Night*', Bobby's dad said. 'It woke us up!'

'And I had no idea you could speak German!' Grumps said. 'Where did you learn that?'

'What time is it?' Bobby asked, remembering the German soldiers singing *Silent Night* and how he had learned the words by singing along.

'Time you got yourself back into bed, young man,' Bobby's mum said.

'I came down because I could hear a noise,'

Bobby explained, then looked at his grandad. 'You had fallen asleep watching a war film, Grumps.'

'And I missed the best bit,' Grumps yawned. 'Where the soldiers all play football. That really happened, too, you know.'

'I know!' Bobby said, his excited words bringing back more memories of what he had experienced with Bill and Noel and all the other soldiers.

Mum clicked her fingers, and pointed Bobby up the stairs to his room.

'I know, Mum!' Bobby said, and after saying good night to everyone, rushed up to his bedroom.

With everyone back in bed, Bobby lay his head down on his pillow, Ruffian snuggled up at his feet. Then, as he turned to go to sleep, something tickled his tummy.

Bobby leapt out of bed.

'There's something in the bed, Ruff!' he said. 'It tickled me!'

Bobby stared as something small moved under his blankets.

'There it is, Ruff!' Bobby shouted. 'What is it?'

'It's me!' squeaked a little voice Bobby recognised.

'Noel?'

From under the blankets came the mouse Bobby had met in the trenches.

'Sorry about that,' Noel said. 'Didn't mean to scare you.'

'But how are you here?' Bobby asked. 'I've never brought anything back with me before, from any of my adventures!'

'Don't ask me,' Noel said. 'I'm just a mouse!'

Bobby climbed back into bed and watched as Noel scurried down towards Ruffian then curled up nice and warm under one of the dog's large, soft ears, pulling it over himself like a blanket.

Bobby lay in bed and smiled. Noel was the proof he needed that at least one of his adventures had been real. And he was so relieved that he had been able to save little Noel from being eaten. He was now a new member of the family. But what about all the other voyages he'd been on? Had they just been dreams? One thing Bobby knew for certain and that was that his first term at school had been full of excitement and fun! And with happy thoughts of his new friends sweeping through his head, Bobby fell into a deep sleep.

When Bobby next awoke, the darkness of his bedroom told him that Christmas morning hadn't quite arrived, not yet. He yawned and stretched and rolled over to go back to sleep when he heard a strange soft dragging sound somewhere in his room.

'Ruff?' Bobby called out. 'Is that you?'

Bobby felt Ruffian's tail thump on his bed, down by his feet. It wasn't the dog then, so what was it? Then he remembered Noel, the mouse.

'Noel? What are you doing?'

'Trying to sleep,' Noel replied in his small voice. 'Which isn't easy if you're going to spend the night talking!'

Bobby lay in his bed, keeping as still as he possibly could, staring into the darkness. Then a shape emerged from the gloom and Bobby held his breath as it loomed over his bed. A laugh bounced into the room, and Bobby knew exactly who it was in the room with him, Ruffian and Noel.

'Santa?'

'Boo!' said Santa, lifting a small candle lamp to shine on his face.

Bobby laughed.

'Budge up, then,' Santa said, sitting down on Bobby's bed. 'Hope you don't mind me waking you to say Happy Christmas!'

'Of course not!' Bobby said.

'Big Daddy Bing, Sage and Onion asked me to say hello as well!' said Santa. 'And this is a little something from us all!'

Bobby saw a small parcel in Santa's hand.

'For me?'

'Of course!' Santa said. Well, open it, then. Come on! I'm very busy, you know!'

Bobby tore open the wrapping paper.

'It's a snow globe!' he said.

'Shake it!' said Santa Claus with a wide grin on his chubby face.

Bobby gave the globe a shake and it lit up in a sea of bright colours, making Bobby close his eyes for a second. He looked into the globe and saw

Dag, Fly, Pip and Dink. Not on Scruff Island, but at home with their owners, all the dogs on their hind legs waving at Bobby.

'Shake it again,' said Santa.

Bobby did as he was told and once again the globe lit up. But this time Bobby saw that the scene had changed.

'It's Harold and his dad!' said Bobby, staring at them both sitting by the piano in their house. They were wearing Christmas party hats and had party blowers. And they looked so happy!

'So, all my adventures were real!' said Bobby,

turning to Santa, but his room was empty, and the jolly bringer of presents had vanished!

Bobby gave the globe another shake and saw Santa in his sleigh shooting across the night sky, being pulled along by his reindeer.

'It's a busy night, Bobby, and I have more presents to deliver!' Santa shouted, turning to look at him from inside the globe. 'Thank you for saving Christmas!'

Bobby climbed back into bed and gave the globe one last shake. Up popped his new gang from school. He couldn't have felt any happier than he did right then. His adventures had all been real and the memories were alive in the snow globe!

Bobby slipped back out of bed and placed the snow globe carefully on the windowsill. Wondering just what other exciting escapades he would soon be having, he shuffled over to join Ruffian and Noel who had both fallen back to sleep on his bed.

With one last look at the snow globe, Bobby slipped back under his blankets then reached out and rested a hand on Ruffian's soft, furry head.

'Happy Christmas!' Bobby whispered, then closed his eyes.

A few minutes later, and sure now that Bobby was asleep, Noel jumped off the bed and crept over to the snow globe. A happy bearded face appeared inside.

'Ah, there you are, Noel!' Santa said. 'I wondered when I would be hearing from you! Everything is going to plan, I assume?'

'Absolutely!' Noel said, giving Santa a little salute. 'And I'll be keeping an eye on him, just like you asked me to!'

'I knew I could trust you,' Santa said. 'Bobby is a very special boy, you know, with a very special voice.'

'That he is, Santa,' Noel said. 'And that he has.'

'Have a Happy Christmas, Noel!' Santa said.

'You, too, Santa,' replied Noel.

Then the snow globe faded and Noel was left in

the dark to scurry back over to where Bobby and Ruffian were fast asleep.

'Happy Christmas, Bobby Dean,' Noel said. 'And sleep well. Because you know what? I think we're going to be having many more adventures very soon indeed!'

And with that, Noel shuffled under one of Ruffian's warm, furry ears, closed his eyes, and fell fast asleep.

Go on more adventures with Bobby Dean!

Coming soon . . .

BOBBY DEAN AND THE GOLDEN EGG
9781529376166 | Hardback | FEB 2022

BOBBY DEAN AND THE UNDERGROUND
KINGDOM
9781529383195 | Hardback | JULY 2022